Queen of the Toilet Bowl

Orca currents

Frieda Wishinsky

ORCA BOOK PUBLISHERS

National Library of Canada Cataloguing in Publication Data

Wishinsky, Frieda
Queen of the toilet bowl / Frieda Wishinsky.

(Orca currents)
ISBN 1-55143-364-8

I. Title. II. Series.

PS8595.I834Q43 2005   jC813'.54   C2005-900788-5

Summary: Renata learns to be proud of who she is.

First published in the United States, 2005
Library of Congress Control Number: 2005921305

Orca Book Publishers gratefully acknowledges the support for its publishing
programs provided by the following agencies: the Government of Canada
through the Book Publishing Industry Development Program (BPIDP), the
Canada Council for the Arts, and the British Columbia Arts Council.

Cover design: Lynn O'Rourke
Cover photography: Getty Images

Orca Book Publishers
PO Box 5626, Stn. B
Victoria, BC Canada
V8R 6S4

Orca Book Publishers
PO Box 468
Custer, WA USA
98240-0468

Printed and bound in Canada.
Printed on 30% post-consumer recycled paper,
processed chlorine-free using vegetable, low VOC inks.

08 07 06 05 • 5 4 3 2 1

*For my friends, Anne, Lynn,
Ronnie and Sydell.*

*And with thanks to
Tauane Machado.*

chapter one

Why was I worried? Liz and I hung around together at school but going to her house made everything different. Going to her house made us real friends.

"Sit down," said Liz. "That is if you can find a place."

I looked around Liz's room. There were mounds of clothes on her bed, a pile of shoes on her floor and books piled on her desk.

"Where?" I asked.

Liz shoved some clothes off her bed. "Here," she said.

I plunked myself down on her pink and red flowered quilt. "Great quilt," I said.

Liz pushed another pile of clothes off her bed and flopped down beside me. "My aunt made it when I was ten." Liz patted her quilt like an old friend. "It has a couple of holes and a mustard stain near the top, but I love it."

"It's beautiful," I said.

"If you could see it," said Liz laughing. "I always plan to clean my room, but things get in the way. It drives my mom crazy. She's a neat freak."

It was true. The rest of Liz's house looked like a movie set. There were sparkling mahogany antique tables, glass lamps and a marble coffee table with four perfectly lined-up glossy magazines on top. It looked like no one ever sat on or touched anything.

"I bet your room is neat," said Liz. "You're so organized."

My tiny bedroom was more like a closet than a room. Liz's bedroom was as big as our living room and kitchen put together. She had space to sprawl out. She had room to be messy, but even the smallest pile of clutter would make my room crowded.

"I'm not that neat," I said.

I didn't want Liz to think I was a neat freak too. Liz and I had known each other for four years, but we'd only become friends since we'd both started grade nine at High Road High. I didn't want anything to spoil that.

"Let's listen to music," said Liz, pulling a CD player out from under her bed.

She popped in a CD and soon she was singing along with the music. She was also laughing and apologizing. "I know my voice stinks," she said. "I can't keep a tune to save my life."

"It's not so bad," I said.

"You don't have to be nice," said Liz. "I don't care if I have a lousy voice. I love to sing."

I used to love to sing too, but I hadn't sung in a long time. To my surprise, I belted out a song like Judy Garland singing "Over the Rainbow." Liz stopped singing and stared at me. "I didn't know you could sing," she said.

"I don't usually," I told her.

"But you should. Your voice is amazing. You should try out for the school play."

"I couldn't sing in front of a whole room full of kids and teachers."

"Yes you could. Try," said Liz.

But I couldn't. I didn't want anyone pointing at me, noticing me, talking about me. It was hard enough being from Brazil in a school where almost no one else came from a foreign country. I wanted to be invisible.

I used to sing all the time in Sao Paolo, where I lived until I was nine. But here it was different. I couldn't sing in public here.

"Liz," called her mom. "I have to go out for an hour. Who was that singing on the radio?"

"That wasn't the radio. It was Renata," said Liz. "Isn't her voice amazing?"

"It's beautiful, Renata," said Liz's mom, standing at the door. Liz's mom smiled warmly at me. She had a small, round face like Liz and short brown hair. Her black pants and white shirt didn't have a single crease or wrinkle.

"I wish you'd clean this room up," she told Liz. "I don't know how you can stand all this clutter."

"It's not clutter," insisted Liz. "Everything in here is special. I'm a collector, Mom. I can't get rid of my stuff. I need all of it."

"There's a fine line between a collection and a pile of junk," said her mother.

"How can you call my stuff junk? It's unique and I love it. Every bit of it."

Liz's mom sighed. You could tell they'd had this discussion before.

"Anyway," said Liz curling her arms around a pillow. "Clutter is my style."

"I wish you'd get a new style," said her mom. Then she turned to go. "See you later, girls. And Renata, you really do have a lovely voice. You should do something with it."

"See," said Liz. "I told you your voice was amazing. Now you have to try out for the school show."

"I can't," I said. "I can't sing in front of anyone else."

"Guess what?" said Liz. "You just did."

chapter two

"Ohmygod! Her mother's a cleaning lady?"

I heard the words first, then the laughter.

I stared into my opened locker. I couldn't move. I couldn't let them find out I was here. I wanted to melt into the darkness inside my locker. I wanted to curl up in the soft cotton of the sweater sprawled across the locker's bottom and stay there until they left. Stay there forever.

I knew the voices. Darleen and Karin. Karin with an i instead of an e, and a smile as tight as a fist. Karin with her straight blond hair and her ring-covered hands. And Darleen, who never left Karin's side, tall and gangly with long, pointy nails.

They were so different from me with my thick bundle of curly black hair and bitten-down nails.

"Where did you hear that?" asked Darleen.

"From my aunt. Renata's mother cleans her house," said Liz.

"How can her mother stand cleaning other people's dirty toilets? I'd rather be shot dead than clean my brother's bathroom. It's not fit for pigs."

"I know," said Liz. "It's disgusting."

Their locker doors slammed shut with a sharp twang.

"Let's go. My mom's picking me up for a dentist appointment," said Karin.

"You have no idea how much I hate the dentist."

I listened as their footsteps echoed down the linoleum floor.

Silence.

I peeked from behind my locker. They were gone. The hall was empty.

I leaned against my locker door and tried to stop shaking. But the shaking wouldn't go away. Not on the bus ride home. Not until I reached our apartment. I'd never told anyone at school what my mom did for a living, and now everyone would know.

Mom was home from her job uptown. I could smell rice and beans simmering on the stove. She was in the kitchen slicing tomatoes.

"Renata, I need you to call one of my ladies for me," she said in Portuguese.

I had to phone people for Mom. Her English was still rusty.

"Who do you want me to call?" I asked.

"Ms. Powell. I can't clean her house

this Friday. I have to take your brother to the doctor for his shot."

I didn't understand why Mom called the women she worked for her "ladies." They weren't "her" ladies. They didn't care about her. She wasn't important to them except to sweep, dust and wash their floors and sinks. Maybe her favorite, Ms. Lucy, cared a little, but the rest didn't. If Mom disappeared off the face of the earth, all they'd worry about was finding another cleaning lady, especially Karin's aunt, Ms. Powell.

I knew before I dialed that Ms. Powell would hate having her schedule changed. "Well," she said, her annoyance crackling through the phone. "If she really has to, I guess I'll just have to manage, but I hope this isn't a regular occurrence."

I imagined her face scrunched up like a prune. Mom said she wasn't so bad, but Mom always said that. That's what made me so angry. Mom never complained.

"We're lucky to be here," she always told me.

I knew we were, but sometimes I missed Sao Paolo. True we had lived in two small, dark rooms and the streets were always crowded with beggars and little kids without shoes. I hated the smell of rotting garbage. Sometimes it hung in the air for days and made me feel sick.

But there was also excitement on festival days. The city buzzed with people singing, dancing and laughing. People helped each other in Sao Paolo. After my father died in a car accident, people I hardly knew came over with food and comforting words.

I missed the sunshine. The sun shone all the time in Sao Paolo. So many days in this new country were dark, dreary and cold. But Mom said there were more opportunities here. We could get a better education here, so I decided to go to High Road High.

I'd had a choice. I could have gone to another high school, the one that was like a little UN with kids from Portugal, Jamaica, Haiti, Pakistan, India and countries I'd never even heard of before. There were a few immigrant kids at High Road High, but they were sprinkled around like raisins in cereal.

I chose this high school because it was better, because there were no gangs roaming the halls. And it was true, there were no gangs of girls with "Go to Hell" tattooed across their backs or snarling guys with knives. But there were gangs of girls with eyes that shut you out and voices that sneered and laughed at you. They didn't beat you up or steal your money, but their looks felt like hard punches to your stomach.

I couldn't tell Mom what I'd overheard at the lockers today. She had enough to deal with. My little brother, Lucas, was a whiny pain. And Mom was always tired.

"I'm going to my room to do home-work," I told her.

"Good," said Mom.

But I didn't start on my homework. I flopped down on my bed and stared at a picture of a butterfly I had snapped for photography class.

I'd seen the butterfly perched on a rose last spring. After I snapped the picture, it flew away.

I wished I was that butterfly. I wished I could fly away.

chapter three

Even though it's a crazy language with weird expressions and insane spellings, I'd learned English quickly.

When I first heard the expression "she laughed her head off" in grade four, I looked around the classroom expecting some bloody head to bounce along the floor. Of course it didn't, and I soon learned to repeat English expressions as if I'd grown up with them.

I'd even lost most of my accent. Whatever I hear, I absorb as if I swallowed it.

Mom was proud of how I'd learned English so quickly. She mentioned it often.

"Sometimes you sound like you were never born in Sao Paolo," she said the next morning at breakfast. "It's because you have a musical ear. I wish you would sing again like you used to in Sao Paolo. I miss your singing."

"Maybe one day I will," I said. It had felt good to sing at Liz's house. It especially felt good when Liz and her mom said they liked my voice.

Liz mentioned it again at lunch.

"You really have a terrific voice," she said. "My mother couldn't stop talking about it last night. Which was great because she stopped talking about my room for an hour."

"Hey. I like your hair," I said, changing the subject. Liz had cut her long curly hair and it circled her face like a frame.

"Thanks," she said. "I hated how short it was yesterday, but now I kind of like it too."

"Fries any good?" I asked.

"Disgusting but the ketchup's good."

Liz and I laughed.

"I keep promising myself to bring something edible from home, but I'm always in such a rush in the morning. Not like you."

"I'm not crazy about the caf food either," I said. It was true, but the real reason I didn't buy my lunch was money. I couldn't afford to buy lunch, even with my new job at the convenience store.

"Hiya Liz," squealed a voice.

Liz and I both looked up. Karin was standing over us with Darleen and Niki beside her.

"Hi Re-na-ta," said Karin, shooting out each syllable like a bullet.

Karin turned to Liz.

"Are you trying out for the play?" she asked. "They're doing *The Sound of Music*."

"I can't sing to save my life," said Liz, "but Renata has a great voice. You should hear her."

"Really?" said Karin, never looking at me. "You know you have to spend a lot of time at rehearsals. Don't you have to help your mother clean people's houses?"

"Not usually," I mumbled.

"Are you trying out, Karin?" asked Liz.

"Yes. I'm taking singing lessons with a well-known vocal teacher. My lessons cost a fortune, but my mother feels it's worth every penny. My teacher works at the conservatory, and she absolutely insists I try out for the play. So I guess I'll have to. See you, Liz," said Karin, ignoring me.

Karin and her friends walked off.

"You really should try out," Liz encouraged me. "Just to show Karin, if nothing else."

"She keeps telling people my mom's a cleaning lady. It's as if she was the queen or something," I said.

"Karin has delusions of grandeur," said Liz. "Ignore her. She's just talk."

I wanted to believe Liz, but I hated the way Karin treated me.

"Maybe I will try out for the play," I said. "It might be fun." The words spilled out before I realized what I was saying.

"I'll go with you," Liz offered. "I might even volunteer to work on the set. I can't sing, but I can paint. And that cute guy, Doug, always works on school plays."

"When are the tryouts, anyway?" I asked.

"Tomorrow after school," Liz answered.

I took a deep breath. "Okay. Let's go."

I immediately regretted my decision. Did I really want to try out? Did I really want to expose myself to everyone's comments?

All day in class, I kept imagining myself on stage while Karin and her gang sat in the seats below. What if my voice cracked, or I froze and couldn't remember the words to the song? Karin would elbow her friends and laugh. "Look at the cleaning lady's daughter. She's so pathetic." No, I thought. I can't let that happen. I'll tell Liz I've changed my mind first thing in the morning.

When I got home, Mom was lying on the couch with a pillow over her eyes.

"A migraine," she groaned. "I thought I'd never get through the day. Could you bring me a cold glass of water, Renata?"

"Sure, but where's Lucas?" I asked.

"At a friend's till nine. Thank goodness."

I knew what Mom meant. The apartment was blissfully quiet without Lucas's booming voice. Lucas was the kind of kid you heard all the time. If he wasn't asking Mom or me a million questions, he was bouncing a ball against his wall or blasting the TV. Sometimes he gave me a headache. And I don't get headaches like Mom does.

After I brought Mom a glass of water, I sat at the kitchen table with my history assignment and an apple, but I couldn't concentrate on either. All I could think about was why I'd agreed to try out for the play. I felt like I was about to walk on a tightrope with no net beneath me.

I knew Karin wanted to be Maria, the lead. But why was she so worried about me? After all, she was taking professional singing lessons. Her teacher said she was good. But I knew my voice was strong. I had a chance against Karin. I wished Liz hadn't told her about my voice. Then she would have left me alone.

I took a bite of my apple. It was sharp and crisp. Maybe I could be like this apple, crisp with bite. Then Karin wouldn't bother me. She wouldn't dare. I'd bite her head off. I laughed as I thought of the words, "bite her head off." What a crazy expression that was!

I wrote a sentence down for my assignment on the reasons for the French Revolution. I knew how the French people felt.

"The French people felt oppressed by the wealthy who cared only for themselves," I wrote.

The French aristocrats were like Karin—confident, only thinking of themselves and looking down on the poor. Maybe they didn't deserve to be guillotined, but they deserved something. After all, poor people were just as important as rich people.

Yes! I decided. I am going to try out for the play. I'll show Karin that I'm just as important as she is.

chapter four

The day started with a thud. I heard it. Then I felt it.

Pain ripped through my head like a hot iron. For an instant I felt dizzy, stunned.

"Are you stupid or something?" a voice shot out. "Don't you look where you're going?"

It was Karin, rubbing her head.

I hadn't been paying attention. I was so absorbed in my thoughts about the tryouts that I hadn't looked where I was going. And now we'd collided.

"Sorry," I muttered.

"My head is killing me. You probably gave me a concussion and all you can say is sorry. You're just a...a..." Karin snarled. I almost apologized again, but I caught myself just in time.

No, I wasn't going to apologize again. I said I was sorry. I hadn't killed her.

"Do you believe her?" I heard Karin tell Darleen as I walked down the hall. "And she thinks she's going to get a part in our school play. No one would cast a loser like her."

I didn't turn. I walked on. No. *Don't let her bother you*, I repeated over and over like a Buddhist mantra.

"Hey Renata," called Liz as I neared my history class. "Are you ready for the tryouts?"

"I don't know if I'm ready," I said, "but I'm going to try."

"You'll knock their socks off," said Liz.

"I hope so," I said. For a minute I pictured a roomful of people with falling socks as I belted out my song. Then I pictured Karin's socks flying right off her skinny legs and circling the earth.

"Meet you after art,"called Liz as she ran to her math class and I walked into history. I sat down, prepared to hear Mr. Brewster talk about Revolution.

Mr. Brewster loved revolution. It didn't matter whose revolution. The American, the French, the Russian. Mr. Brewster rattled off revolutionary facts, especially the gory facts, like an almanac. He knew how many aristocrats died in the French Revolution. He knew how many people starved at Valley Forge with George Washington in the American Revolution. He knew all the theories of what might have happened to the Czar's family during the Russian Revolution. And none of his theories were pretty.

"Mankind needs revolution to cleanse itself of injustices," he began as soon as class started, "but each revolution has a price, often paid by the innocent."

As he spoke, I pictured Karin rattling along in a cart on her way to the guillotine. I could almost hear the rumble of drums, the clip clop of the horse, the leers and cheers of the mob.

"Come back! Come Back, Renata," said Mr. Brewster. "I asked you to read the opening lines from Dickens' *A Tale of Two Cities* and you haven't even opened your book."

"I'm sorry," I muttered. I was apologizing again! This whole day was turning into one big fat apology.

I opened the book and took a deep breath.

"It was the best of times. It was the worst of time. It was..."

Dickens understood how I felt. It would be the best of times if I got a good part in the play and the worst of times if Karin got the lead and rubbed it in.

"Well read," said Mr. Brewster. "Those words express the complexity of the French Revolution. They touch on how complicated life can be when both good and bad forces compete."

I'd know soon enough if it was the best or worst of times. Would I get a part in the play, or would I freeze like an icicle at the tryouts? Only four more hours and I'd know.

The time seemed to fly and drag at the same time and then, suddenly, there I was sitting beside Liz, waiting for my turn to audition.

Sure enough Karin and her friends were sitting behind Liz and me. And sure enough they whispered and pointed at each person who tried out. I could hear their comments. "She hasn't got a chance," and "Did you see how fat her stomach is" and "Pimple Boy will never get a part with that face."

It was Karin's turn. She shimmied on stage.

"Break a leg!" shouted Darleen.

Another crazy English expression I had never understood. Why was it good to break a leg?

Karin smiled broadly at Ms. Watson, the drama teacher and her friends, and then she began to sing.

She sang confidently. And she hadn't been lying. She had a good voice, maybe not a great voice and not a voice with a lot of feeling but good enough for a part.

When Karin finished singing, she turned and faced the audience as if waiting for applause. She got it. Her two friends clapped and clapped. Karin bowed as if she had just received a ten minute standing ovation from an audience of a thousand. Then she slowly walked off the stage.

As she passed me, she glanced down. "Your turn," she said.

"Renata," said Ms. Watson.

I tried standing up but my legs wouldn't move. They were shaky and weak. "Go on, Renata," whispered Liz, giving me a nudge. "Knock their socks off!"

I tried standing up again. This time I stood, but my legs felt as tired as if I'd run a marathon.

I walked on stage. I tried not to look at Karin and her friends, but I couldn't ignore their laughter.

Don't let them bother you, I told myself over and over in my new mantra.

"Ready?" said Ms. Watson.

"Ready," I stammered.

Ms. Watson began to play the piano.

chapter five

My voice croaked. I cleared my throat and tried again but out stumbled another croak. Laughter rippled from the audience. My face flushed. I wanted to sink though the floor.

Ms. Watson handed me a glass of water.

"Thanks," I said, gulping it down.

"Ready?" said Ms. Watson.

"Ready," I answered.

Slow down. Slow down I told myself as she began to play. You'll be okay. You will. You will...

I opened my mouth again and sang "Climb Every Mountain." My voice exploded, crisp and strong, and I forgot about Karin. I forgot about her friends. I forgot about everything except the music and the words. And then it was over.

I glanced at Ms. Watson. She was beaming. I beamed back. I floated off stage and dropped into the seat beside Liz.

"You were amazing," said Liz, squeezing my hand.

"Really?" I said.

"Look at Karin's face and you'll know you were amazing," Liz whispered.

I glanced at Karin. Her face was wrinkled into a scowl. I had never seen her that angry. She looked like she might burst into a thousand small pieces.

Ten more singers tried out, some good, some mediocre and one so bad that I couldn't believe she had the guts to get up and sing. But she was so good-natured and funny that despite her off-key, creaky voice, everyone laughed with her.

"Do you know her well? I've only spoken to her a few times," I told Liz.

"Yeah," said Liz, "She's a goof but a good goof."

"I like her," I said.

So did Ms. Watson. "Cheryl, you may not be the best singer in the world, but you have enormous stage presence," Ms. Watson commented when Cheryl finished. "We may find a spot for you in the show after all."

Then Ms. Watson turned to the rest of us. "I'll post the parts on the bulletin board outside the office tomorrow morning. Thanks for trying out."

Ms. Watson gathered her music and left. Karin and her two friends followed her out.

"See," said Liz as we walked out. "Karin knows the score now. She'll have to live with it. You're bound to get a great part, maybe even the part of Maria. Think of it, Renata, you might get the lead!"

I knew I had a crack at the part of Maria and I knew Karin was going to hate it.

All evening at home, my stomach knotted so tightly I could hardly eat.

"Can I have your rice?" asked Lucas.

"Sure," I said. "I'm not hungry."

"How about your apple pie?" asked Lucas.

"Fine," I said. "Take the whole thing."

"Renata, you have to eat something," said Mom.

"I have no appetite," I said. "Tomorrow they announce the people who have parts in *The Sound of Music*."

"I don't know why you want to be in a dumb musical anyway," said Lucas. "I hate movies where people sing. Now if you were doing a car chase that would be cool."

"Musicals can be very beautiful," said Mom. "If Renata gets a part, it will be a great honor. I will be very proud."

I tossed and turned for hours that night. I kept checking the time. Twelve AM. One AM. I have to get some sleep I kept thinking, but the more I thought about sleep, the slower it came. Images of me as Maria in *The Sound of Music* danced through my head. Images of Karin laughing at me danced alongside them.

I tried my new mantra a dozen times. *Don't let her bother you. Don't let her bother you.* And finally it must have worked because the next thing I knew it was morning.

I caught the bus and ran the two blocks to school. I wanted to get to the bulletin board before a big crowd gathered. I wanted to see the posting before Karin and her friends arrived. But I was too late. Karin was in the front row.

chapter six

"Hurrah. I'm a nun!" shouted Cheryl.

There were so many kids huddled around the bulletin board, I couldn't see a thing.

"Hey, you're a nun too and you're also the lead's understudy," Cheryl told Karin.

"Great," said Karin, sarcastically.

Cheryl ignored the acid in Karin's voice.

"I always liked the nuns' parts. It's

going to be so much fun acting in the play," said Cheryl.

"Maybe for you," said Karin. "Ms. Watson is *so* ridiculous. I hear she often gives out good parts to people she feels sorry for. Who does she think she is, some kind of saint? It's so stupid to ruin the play with mediocre talent."

I knew then, as if it had been announced over a loud speaker or lit up in blazing neon, that I had the part of Maria. I wanted to leap up and dance, but there was no room in the thick crowd to even wiggle.

"Hey, Liz's friend Renata is Maria," said Cheryl. "That's cool."

"Cool?" said Karin. "It's pathetic." Then Karin pushed her way out of the crowd and stomped off.

"Did you hear that Renata?" said Liz, elbowing me excitedly. "You're Maria! You got the part!"

"Come on," I said as kids drifted to class and the crowd thinned out. "I want to see this with my own eyes."

We still had to tiptoe to see over Pat Pomeroy and Lenore White's heads, but at least I could read the first line and that's where it was.

Renata Nunes–Maria von Trapp

"Yes!" I shouted, high-fiving Liz.

"Hey congratulations," said Lenore and Pat in front of me.

"Thanks," I said.

I couldn't wait to tell Mom, but I couldn't call her at work. She was at Ms. Powell's today. Ms. Powell didn't like personal calls at her house, and Mom didn't have a cell phone yet.

The rest of the day was a dream. Kids who didn't know I existed before said "Hi, Renata" and "Congratulations." Ms. Watson stopped me in the hall and said, "I knew as soon as I heard you sing that you were perfect for Maria."

I wanted to hug her, but all I could sputter was, "Thank you. I'm really happy."

And I was happier than I'd been all year.

At the end of the day I ran to my locker, eager to get home and tell Mom about the part. I was slipping on my jacket when I heard Karin.

"My new watch is gone!" she screamed. "I took it off at lunch because the band was making my arm itchy. I left it on the shelf in my locker but I was in such a hurry, I must have left my locker unlocked. And now it's gone. Someone took it. It cost a fortune. It's a designer watch."

"That's terrible," said Darleen. "Who could have taken it?"

"I bet I know who took it."

"Who?" asked Darleen.

"That Renata something or other. You know the one whose mother is a cleaning lady. I saw her hovering around my locker at lunch. Of course, I didn't think anything of it then but now. Now..."

"You don't think she really took it?" asked Darleen. "She'd be in such trouble and maybe get expelled. And she just got the part of Maria in the play."

"There was absolutely no one else around. She must have seen me take the watch off and put it on the shelf," said Karin. "And she's sneaky. You can see it in her eyes. She's probably sold my watch already."

"She seems shy to me," said Darleen.

"Shy? You've got to be kidding," said Karin. "If she's so shy, she wouldn't have tried out for the play and shown off like that in the auditorium. Just because she sings loud, doesn't mean she sings well."

My heart pounded as Karin droned on. I couldn't move. I hid behind my locker door and prayed they'd go away.

I hadn't been anywhere near Karin's locker at lunch. I'd been in the library the whole time, but no one saw me. The helper never looked up from the computer, and Ms. Dunn wasn't there until the last fifteen minutes.

I had no alibi. It was Karin's word against mine.

chapter seven

"Renata, I'm so proud," said Mom.

Her face was glowing. I hadn't seen her so happy since the day she got the papers allowing us to stay in our new country.

"I wish your grandparents were alive to see you. You know Grandma had a lovely voice like you."

Mom was always telling me stories of how Grandpa fell in love with Grandma when he heard her sing from the balcony of her apartment. She made it sound like a scene from *Romeo and Juliet*.

Both my grandparents died three years ago. Mom never forgave herself for not being there, but they both had sudden heart attacks a week apart.

"I will buy a special dress to go to the play," said Mom, "and I will buy Lucas a new shirt and pants."

"I don't want to dress up," complained Lucas. "What's wrong with my black pants?"

"Just three holes and a ripped seam," I said.

"I like it that way. It's cool," said Lucas. Cool was Lucas's favorite word.

I didn't tell Mom about Karin's accusations. I had tried all evening to block Karin's words out of my mind. I hoped they'd just blow away like a storm.

"I'll be late tonight. Rehearsals start today," I told Mom the next morning.

"Boa Sorte. Good luck," she told me in Portuguese and English as she scurried around making beds and lunches. Then she was out the door with Lucas.

I nibbled my Cornflakes and imagined myself on stage, my voice filling every corner of the auditorium. I imagined the audience hushed like in a cathedral, listening to me sing. I imagined Mom in the front row, beaming like she'd just won the lottery.

I stood up to refill my bowl, when I noticed the clock. Nuts! I only had a few minutes to catch the bus. I was huffing like an old broken-down engine, when I slid into my seat in history. Mr. Brewster walked in a minute later.

"Your assignment on the French Revolution is due next week," he reminded us.

Then he began to talk about Queen Marie Antoinette of France. He told us how privileged her life had been compared to the lives of peasants in France. He told us that she never said those famous words, "Let them eat cake," when she was told that the peasants had no bread. He told us that she wasn't evil but was caught up in rumors and the revolution that was sweeping across France. He asked us if we thought she behaved in an aristocratic manner because of the way she was brought up.

Donald Defoe waved his hand in the air before Mr. Brewster was finished.

"She wasn't blind," said Donald. "She lived in a palace, not on the moon. She had to know people were starving. Being brought up rich is no excuse."

"Maybe she just didn't know what to do," said Jennifer McRae. "Maybe she didn't have enough power as queen. After all, in those days the King was in charge."

"All good points to consider," said Mr. Brewster. "When you go home, read about the diamond necklace affair, and then tomorrow we can talk about how rumors can flourish and destroy people's lives. Even the lives of queens."

Mr. Brewster got us all buzzing about Marie Antoinette. I hadn't thought much about her before. I knew that she was the queen who was beheaded during the French Revolution, but what kind of person was she? And what was this whole business about rumors?

I was certainly getting to know a lot about that subject, although I hoped Karin's rumor wouldn't get me beheaded.

"Renata Nunes. Please come to the office at lunch." Ms. Bartlett's crisp, officious voice blasted over the intercom.

My heart almost stopped. What was that about? I'd never been called to the office before. Had something happened to Mom or Lucas? Or had Karin told the principal I stole her watch? If it was about Mom or Lucas, I probably would have been asked to go to the office immediately rather than at lunch. It had to be about Karin. Why did she have to make my life so miserable? She had a good life, a big house and friends. What did she need to hassle me for?

There was still fifteen minutes left in class, so I said my *don't let her bother you* mantra twice and tried to pay attention to the debate about Marie Antoinette. But this time nothing worked. I didn't care about Marie Antoinette. I didn't care about anything except what I was going to encounter in the office and what I would I say.

All I had was the truth, but was the truth enough? Certainly not enough to prevent me from getting in trouble. Certainly not enough to stop the whole school from talking about me. Possibly not enough to let me keep what I now wanted most of all—to be Maria in the play.

chapter eight

"Renata," said Mr. Bowman slowly, as if he was counting each word. "I called you into the office because of a complaint made by another student. Karin Walters' watch is missing, and she claims you stole it. She says she saw you in the vicinity of her locker at the time she inadvertently left her locker open. As I said to Karin, that is circumstantial evidence at best, but I feel it's my duty to speak to you about the matter."

"I didn't take her watch," I blurted out.

"I understand this is distressing to you," said Mr. Bowman. "It distresses me too. You have no record of misbehavior, but I must tell you Karin was quite convinced of your guilt."

Mr. Bowman was distressed! Ha! It wasn't his neck on the line. He didn't care about me. I remembered how abrupt he was when I first registered at the school with Mom.

"Will you be able to arrive at school on time?" he had asked me then. "The school is some distance from your... apartment." He knew we weren't part of the upscale neighborhood the school was located in.

"I'll be on time," I had barked at him. Mom said she could hear the anger in my voice.

"You have to be careful," she cautioned me when we left his office. "When you're poor and an immigrant you have to be especially careful of your behavior. People make judgments."

"I don't care," I told her defiantly. "He can think whatever he wants. I have every right to go to this school. Just as much right as the rich kids."

Despite my words I knew Mom was right. It just wasn't fair. Why did people judge Karin and me differently? If I had accused Karin with no evidence would Karin be hauled into the office? Or would Mr. Bowman assume that because her family has money that she wouldn't possibly steal?

Just because you have money doesn't mean you won't steal. What about those heads of companies who take huge salaries and bonuses when their companies are losing money and lower level employees are being fired? Isn't that stealing? The newspapers were full of stories about people like that. What about famous actresses who shoplift? They don't need the stuff they take, but they take things anyway.

"I accept your words," said Mr. Bow-man, "but I can't close the matter yet. Stealing is a serious offense. If you have anything more to tell me on the subject, I hope you will."

"I don't," I said. I knew I sounded angry, but I couldn't help it. Mr. Bowman thought I was guilty and that I needed to confess. How dare he?

"Good day to you then," he said, dismissing me.

I walked out shaking, less because of Karin than because of Mr. Bowman. To him, I was half-guilty just because Karin had accused me.

Perhaps I should have told him why Karin wanted to get me in trouble. But I had no evidence, just a feeling that Karen wanted me out of the play so she could have my part. How could anyone be that awful? A wave of anger hit me so hard I felt nauseous. Suddenly I wanted to run away from school. I wanted to hide from the people, accusing me with the look in their eyes. I knew that Karin was not going to give up.

It sounded like a plot in a movie. Maybe it was a movie. Only I wished I wasn't starring in it.

chapter nine

I sat at the kitchen table and put down the book about Marie Antoinette and the French Revolution I'd just read. It threw everything I believed out the window.

Marie Antoinette was hated not just because she was a rich aristocrat but because she was a foreigner—an Austrian princess married to the French King.

Marie Antoinette even dressed more simply so she wouldn't be considered frivolous and flighty, but the French people still hated her. What really sealed her fate, though, were vicious rumors, especially the diamond necklace affair Mr. Brewster had mentioned.

A Cardinal de Rohan got mixed up with a con artist, Madame La Motte, who pretended to be Marie Antionette. Madame La Motte told the Cardinal that she (the queen) wanted a very expensive necklace. The Cardinal wanted to gain the queen's favor, so he bought the necklace and gave it to Madame La Motte, assuming Marie Antionette would pay for it.

Of course, Marie Antoinette knew nothing about the necklace, and Madame La Motte had no intention of paying for it. Instead Madame La Motte gave the necklace to her con artist husband who sold it in London.

When the truth finally came out, Madame La Motte was arrested, imprisoned, and even flogged and branded. Eventually she escaped to London where she spread nasty rumors about Marie Antoinette. Although it was proven in court that Marie Antoinette had nothing to do with the whole business, the people in France still believed she was guilty. The mob dragged her to the guillotine. She faced her fate bravely, but they still hated her and then they beheaded her.

The more I read, the more I worried. Marie Antoinette was a queen, and even she was powerless to stop false rumors. If she couldn't, how could I? I knew that once the rumor genie is out of the bottle, it's hard to stuff it back in.

I was sure that I, not Karin, was going to be dragged to the guillotine.

I was sure that Karin, not I, was going to lead the crowd in chanting, "Off with her head."

Stop! I thought. Don't make yourself crazy. You are not Marie Antoinette. This is not eighteenth century France. No one is going to cut your head off. Maybe not, but they were going to try to make my life miserable. And they had no right.

By the time Mom and Lucas arrived home I had calmed down, but the worry still nagged at me. I didn't say anything to them. I couldn't worry Mom, and Lucas was too immature to talk to about anything important. I needed someone I could trust.

Liz! I dialed her number, but the answering machine was on. I didn't leave a message.

It was a long, long night of tossing and turning again. The clock kept ticking the hours away as I tried not to think. I must have finally fallen asleep, but when I woke up my head felt like it was full of cotton. The thought of going to school made me feel nauseous again. I drank some water, but the nausea lingered like bad breath.

You did nothing, I told myself on the bus. There's nothing to be ashamed of. You're innocent. Act innocent. Don't feel embarrassed.

By the time I walked the two blocks to school, I felt more in control. But the minute I walked into the school building, I knew everyone was staring at me. All the way to my locker I could feel everyone's eyes on me.

I was sure Karin had told everyone about her watch.

I walked to my locker, trying not to look at anyone. My hands shook as I opened my locker door.

"Hi Renata."

I spun around. It was Liz.

"I guess you know what Karin's saying," said Liz gently.

"Yes," I replied. "Is it all over the school?"

"Every corner," said Liz, "but not everyone believes her. I don't."

A lump stuck in my throat. Oh Liz, I thought. I couldn't say anything for a minute.

"I didn't take the watch," I finally mumbled.

"I know that. You couldn't, but you need to figure out what to do. Karin's on a rampage."

The bell rang. I almost jumped. "Sorry," I said. "This whole thing makes me..."

"Crazy?" said Liz.

"Yes," I said.

"We can talk more at lunch," said Liz, squeezing my hand. Then she ran off to her class.

I walked down the hall to my class. The walls in the hall felt narrow and tight like I was walking in a box with razor-sharp edges. I tried not to pay attention, but I could see the looks on people's faces. I could hear their whispers.

I wanted to run out of the building, but my legs wouldn't let me. And suddenly my anger wouldn't either.

How dare Karin do this, I thought. I can't let her get away with this, but what can I do?

I drifted through the morning as if I was walking through a fog. I took notes. I listened. I kept my eyes firmly on my books, but I was shaking inside.

Finally it was lunch. I passed Karin's table, but I didn't look down. She ignored me.

"Thanks again, Liz," I said as I slid into the seat beside her at lunch.

"For what?" asked Liz, biting into her tuna sandwich.

"For believing me. For not running to the other side of the caf, for... "

"Come on. We're friends. Of course I believe you. And I know Karin. Last year she borrowed my notes for a history essay and our essays were almost identical. Of course she denied it when the teacher called us on it. She even hinted that it might be my fault."

"Wow," I said relieved that Liz knew how sneaky and mean Karin could be. "But you seem to get along with her. She doesn't bother you the way she bothers me."

"I'm not sure why. She likes to vary her victims, and I guess I wasn't juicy enough for her."

"But I am."

"Not because of your personality but because, well, you know, you're from Brazil and you're talented. Karin smells an opportunity to be Maria in the show and you're the only one standing in her way."

chapter ten

They were whispering, but I heard every word. I was in a study carrel at the back of the library reading about Marie Antoinette. I knew they couldn't see me.

"She took it?" said one of them.

"Yes. Karin saw something shiny sticking out of her bag. She's sure it's her watch. She says Renata's been eyeing it all week."

"Does the principal know?"

"He called her down to the office. Karin says she'll probably be suspended. Karin said her mother thinks they should call the police and search her apartment. My mother would kill me if she found out I stole anything."

"Do you think she's a thief?"

"I don't know. She looks normal, but who knows. Karin says she's poor and will do anything to get what she wants. Karin said Ms. Watson felt sorry for her and that's why she gave her the part of Maria in the play."

"I bet she'll lose the part now."

"Yeah. I'm glad I'm not her."

I wanted to shout at them. I wanted to tell them they didn't know anything about me or the watch. I wanted to scream Karin is a liar. She's making things up just to get me in trouble. I wanted to shout at them so much it hurt, but I just sat silently as if I was frozen.

Finally I heard chairs scrape against the floor. Then quiet. I peeked out. The librarian was alone, stamping returned books. I grabbed my coat and raced out the library, out the school and all the way home. Halfway home it started to drizzle, but I didn't care.

I didn't care about anything that night, but when I woke up the next morning I felt different. I was determined to say something about Karin. Someone had to believe me.

"Hi Renata," said Cheryl, as I stuffed my jacket into my locker. "Did you hear about Karin's watch?"

"Yes," I said, ready for Cheryl to tell me more nasty accusations Karin had made about me.

"Then you know I found it," said Cheryl.

"What?"

I spun around.

"It was in her locker the whole time. I saw it in a corner when she asked me to hold her books so she could get her gym clothes."

Relief flooded over me. "Oh," was all I could dribble out.

"Karin wasn't thrilled that I found her watch even though she made such a fuss about it being lost," said Cheryl. "And it wasn't even a real designer watch. My mom bought a watch just like it at the airport for fifteen dollars. Anyway, Karin just picked it up, stuffed it into her pocket, grabbed her books out of my hand and slammed her locker shut. It was weird." Cheryl laughed. "I guess she can't say you took it now."

"No," I said, laughing with relief. "Thanks."

"See you," said Cheryl.

Just then Liz ran over. "Did you hear?" she said, hugging me. "Thank goodness for Cheryl."

I nodded. "But what next? Karin still wants my part."

"She's still just the understudy," said Liz. "All you have to do is be sure you don't get sick and you're fine."

"I won't get sick," I told her. "And even if I do, I'm going to be in that play, no matter what. Even if I break both my arms and legs, I'm going to be Maria. Even if they have to carry me out in my bed. I'm going to be on that stage, singing my guts out."

Liz laughed. "I can see it now. Two strong men will lift you across the stage. The audience will applaud as you are brought in, weak but determined to go on. It will be dramatic. It will be heartwrenching. It will be..."

"A showstopper!" I said, laughing.

In a minute Liz and I were laughing so much we couldn't stop. Tears rolled down our cheeks. Our stomachs shook.

It felt so good to laugh.

"We have our first rehearsal after school today," I said after dabbing my eyes with a crumpled tissue I found wedged in a pocket of my jeans.

"I've volunteered to help with the props and painting," said Liz.

"Will you be at rehearsals today?"

"Yep. Me and that cute guy Doug, and Rob and Bea, and maybe Lucy."

The lunch bell rang.

"We'd better go. See ya!" called Liz.

"See ya."

Maybe finally things will calm down, I thought as I walked to my next class. Maybe Karin will leave me alone.

Then I felt a sharp jab on my shoulder. "Hey!" I said, turning around.

It was Karin.

"You think you're so smart but you're a stupid loser," she snarled.

"And you're just my understudy," I said, walking away. I knew my words would only make her more furious and probably meaner, but I didn't care. I felt like I'd won a gold medal at the Olympics.

chapter eleven

Rehearsals began on time. Ms. Watson was a stickler for punctuality. "Think of yourselves as professionals," she told us. "And professionals show up on time."

To prove her point, when Randall Jones sauntered in twenty minutes late in the middle of my reading, she barked, "If you're late again, Randall, you're out. Go on, Renata. Keep reading."

So I did, and so did everyone else. As we read, Ms. Watson said things like, "More expression. Slow down! Pump it up. Terrific. Keep that tone. Louder. "

To Randall she said, "Remember you're a Nazi. Not a saint. Give us your meanest look and voice."

"Yes ma'am," said Randall and his tone immediately turned nastier.

As for me, Ms. Watson said, "Louder, Renata. Don't be afraid to let your voice out. Fill this auditorium." So I tried, and when I did, Karin giggled and poked her neighbor as if I'd just burped in public. I wanted to tape her mouth shut.

But then something happened. Suddenly I didn't care. Suddenly I felt that Karin couldn't hurt me. The whole watch incident was over. And I loved being on stage. I felt like I owned the auditorium. I felt like a Broadway star.

"That's the way," Ms. Watson said when I finished singing "Climb Every Mountain." Ms. Watson was smiling and nodding. I smiled back.

"Ms. Watson," Karin called out.

"Yes," said Ms. Watson.

"Who'll take my part if, by some unfortunate circumstance, Renata can't be here on opening night and I have to take her part?"

"Good question," said Ms. Watson. "How about you, Liz?"

"Me?" said Liz. "I can't sing."

"You can mouth the words. The other nuns will carry you. Just memorize Karin's lines."

"I can memorize," said Liz, "as long as I don't have to sing."

So there it was. Karin was my understudy, and Liz was Karin's understudy.

"Rehearsal tomorrow. Same time. Same place. Be on time," Ms. Watson shot Randall a sharp look.

"Yes ma'am," he saluted, clicking his heels together Nazi style.

"As for all of you, start memorizing your lines," said Ms. Watson. "You can still read from the script but begin to learn the words. Make them your own.

We only have a month until show time. Let's make every rehearsal count."

"Wanna get together on the weekend?" Liz asked me on our way out. "We can rehearse our lines together."

"Sure," I said.

"I could come over to your place on Saturday morning. My mom's dropping my brother off at karate near you," said Liz.

"I...well...sure," I said, regretting my words as soon as they popped out. Liz had never been to our apartment. What would she think of it? It was small and cramped. Mom slept on a pull-out couch in the living room. Lucas and I had two minuscule rooms and all of our furniture was Salvation Army meets dollar store. Mom dressed things up the best she could and it was clean and neat, except for Lucas's room, but you couldn't miss the chipped stove, the ancient fridge and the burn marks on the kitchen counter. Mom had complained to the landlord, but he didn't care.

"Lady," he said, "you got cheap rent. What do you expect, the Waldorf?"

But how could I tell Liz not to come to my apartment. How could I say I wished we lived better?

chapter twelve

"I'll be at your place at two o'clock on Saturday. Is that okay?" asked Liz.

"Two is fine," I agreed. "See ya."

I tried not to worry about our apartment that night, although I did tell Lucas that he'd better clean the junk off his bed or I'd never forgive him.

"Yeah, yeah, yeah," said Lucas. He made a half-hearted attempt at shoving his baseball, books and action figures into a corner.

Saturday afternoon Mom baked my favorite cookies, biscoito de nata. The smell of butter and sugar filled the apartment like perfume.

Liz arrived fifteen minutes late.

"Hi," she said breathlessly. "We got lost. I thought you lived three blocks down. But anyway, here we are."

I introduced Liz's mom to my mom and they smiled at each other. Liz's mom didn't blink an eye at how our apartment looked. She just said, "I'll come and pick you up in three hours, Liz. Have fun girls."

"Hey, this is neat," said Liz, running over to a wall hanging Mom had brought back from Brazil. "I love the colors."

"Thank you," said Mom.

Liz and I plopped down on my bed. "Cool blanket," said Liz. "Is it from Brazil too?"

"Yes," I answered.

"So has Karin said anything to you since the watch thing?" asked Liz.

"Not for a week. She's been weirdly quiet," I said.

"Maybe she's over her jealousy," said Liz. "Maybe she's accepted the fact that she's not Maria and you are."

"Maybe," I said. "She did give me half a smile on Friday when I passed her in the hall. True, it was like a queen smiling at her lowly subject, but it was better than her usual sneer."

"Yes. A half-smile from Karin is like a year's worth of smiles from anyone else," said Liz. "Maybe playing a nun has improved her personality."

"Fat chance," I said, laughing at another one of those goofy English expressions. "What does 'fat chance' mean anyway?"

"I have no idea," said Liz. "All I know is, we'd better start rehearsing. I think I have Karin's lines down pat now. Although I really don't want to say them or sing."

"Down pat? Who is Pat?" I asked.

"Renata," said Liz, poking me in the side. "Come on. We could spend all day talking about crazy English expressions. We'd better rehearse or we'll be..."

"Dead ducks?" I said.

"Absolutely. Totally. Completely dead ducks."

Liz and I rehearsed for the next two hours. We also ate biscoito de nata.

"I love these cookies," said Liz. "What's in them, anyway?"

"Oh the usual flour, sugar, eggs, milk."

"My mom never bakes anything," said Liz. "She doesn't want to mess up her oven. She thinks grease and stains are a sin."

"Your mom's nice," I said.

"Yeah. She's okay despite her neatness obsession. So's yours," said Liz, her mouth full of biscoito. "And pretty too."

My mom pretty? I'd never thought of her in that way. She was just my mom. "Does your mom diet?" asked Liz. "My mom's a diet nut. She's always worried she's gained two pounds. We own every diet book ever written, and my mom's tried every one of them. You don't know how horrible it was living with the egg and grapefruit diet. I will never eat another egg or grapefruit again. But the worst diet had to be the hot pepper diet. I think the idea was to burn your tongue so you'd never eat again."

"But your mom's not fat," I said.

"Tell that to her. She wants to be size two. Who wants a size two mother?"

"Come on. Let's rehearse," I said laughing.

We read through the script once more.

"We should practice the songs," Liz suggested.

"Okay," I said and I began to sing. As I did, Mom came in and listened. After my second song, Lucas banged on my door. "Pipe down," he shouted. "I can't hear the TV with all that racket."

"It's singing. Not racket," said Liz.

"And it's beautiful," said Mom in Portuguese.

"Who cares?" said Lucas.

"I care," said Mom. "And I don't want to hear another word from you." Mom shot him an annoyed look. Then she turned to us. "Would you and Liz like some hot chocolate?" Mom asked me.

"Absolutely," said Liz, after I translated.

"Hey, can I have some too?" said Lucas, opening the door.

"Only if I hear no more complaints," said Mom.

"No more," said Lucas, "but I wish Renata would learn rap instead of that dumb girlie music."

And with that, Lucas popped back into the living room.

"The hot chocolate should keep him quiet for a while," Mom reassured me.

"For awhile? Maybe for five minutes, if we're lucky," I said.

chapter thirteen

Three weeks of nothing from Karin. Even I was beginning to believe she'd decided to stop hassling me. It wasn't that she was friendly. She ignored me, but at least she didn't accuse me of anything. And if she was bad-mouthing me, at least it was behind my back and no one told me about it. As a matter of fact, a lot of kids who never talked to me before were saying hi.

Rehearsals continued after school every day. Randall was kicked out for being late again and Adam took his place. Rita broke her leg and was replaced by Mandy because she had a dancing part. Karin knew her lines perfectly and Liz flirted like crazy with Doug while she painted a mountain.

"In one week, we're on," said Ms. Watson on Friday. "Most of you have your lines down fairly well, but by Monday, I want them perfect. Costumes will be ready Wednesday, and Thursday is our dress rehearsal. Have a good weekend."

"Do you want to get together again on the weekend?" I asked Liz.

"Sure. Saturday? Your place?'

"You know my brother Lucas will be there," I said.

"I don't mind him. He's actually kind of cute in an annoying little brother way," said Liz. "He's no worse than my pesky brother."

"My brother cute? Yeah right," I said, laughing.

"Well maybe he's not cute but he doesn't bother me," said Liz. "Do you think your mother might be baking those amazing cookies again?"

"Liz," I said. "Are you telling me you like me for my mother's cookies?"

"Yep," said Liz, waving goodbye. "See you Saturday."

I smiled all the way home. It was great having Liz for a friend. It was great being Maria in the play. I never realized how good it would feel to be on stage. I loved singing in front of people. I loved being someone else for a while.

"What are you smiling about?" asked Lucas when I opened the door.

"Nothing," I said, "Where's Mom?"

"At that Ms. Powell's place. She needed Mom to work extra hours. She's having some kind of fancy party tomorrow night and wants Mom to help clean and get everything ready. Boy, is Ms. Powell bossy. I had to call to ask Mom about a school trip and Ms.

Powell screamed at me like I'd broken into her house."

Mom came home at ten. Her eyes were puffy and she hobbled to the couch.

"I am so tired," she said. "I am almost too tired to eat, but I am hungry. Renata, could you make me a sandwich?'

"Cheese and tomato, okay?" I asked.

"Perfect," said Mom, stretching her feet out on the couch. "I don't know if I can work for Ms. Powell anymore. She wants too much from me."

"What do you mean?" I asked.

"I scrubbed her place until it shone, but she still wanted more. She sees dust where it doesn't exist."

"It must be some big party she's having," I said.

"It's a birthday party for her sister, a fancy sister who lives in a big house with her two daughters. I think one of Ms. Powell's nieces goes to your school. Maybe you know her. Her name is Kara or Kari or..."

"Karin?" I asked.

"Yes. That's it. Ms. Powell says Karin is very talented. She sings like you. She even takes singing lessons from a famous teacher. I saw her for a minute when she brought over some decorations for the party. A nice-looking girl. Do you know her well?"

"Not well, but I know her. She's my understudy in the play."

"Ah," said Mom. "That explains why she gave me such a strange look, like a doctor examining a patient."

"Was she rude to you?" I asked Mom, as I handed her the sandwich.

"She was polite, but she had such cold eyes. Ah Renata, thank you, this is a good sandwich. Just what I need."

"Mom, Liz is coming on Saturday so we can practice together. Could you make biscoite de nata again? She loves it."

"I am happy to make it. After a warm bath and a good sleep, I will get up refreshed and bake. I like your friend Liz."

"Me too," I said.

chapter fourteen

Liz came on Saturday and, except for Lucas bouncing his ball against the wall for ten minutes, everything went smoothly.

Mom even made extra biscoite for Liz to take home.

"Oh, Ms. Nunes," said Liz, giving Mom a hug. "You are the best. I'd ask you for your recipe, but my Mom never bakes."

"Maybe you can bake one day," said Mom in English. I stared at her. It was the first time I'd heard my mom speak English to one of my friends. She was usually too embarrassed and worried she'd make a mistake.

"Maybe I can," said Liz. "Maybe you could teach me?"

"Yes," said Mom, beaming.

Liz smiled. "My parents are coming to the play. Is your husband coming too?"

"My husband was killed right after Lucas was born," said Mom. "A car accident."

"Oh, I'm sorry," said Liz. "I... I didn't know. Renata never said. I'm really sorry."

"It was a long time ago," said Mom. "I am okay."

"You're more than okay, Ms. Nunes," said Liz. "See you on Friday."

I wanted to hug Liz for liking my mother, but suddenly I felt as shy as if it was the first day of school. "See you on Monday," I said instead.

I did my homework on Sunday, watched a mystery on TV and went to bed. As I closed my eyes, I pictured myself standing on stage and singing. I pictured rows and rows of people listening and smiling and clapping. I pictured myself bowing and accepting a bouquet of roses.

"Please. Please," I said out loud. "Let it all work out. Let me remember my lines. Let me sing better than I've ever sung before."

The next thing I knew I was staring at my alarm in horror. It was morning and I hadn't heard the alarm. I zoomed out of bed, tossed on some clothes, threw an apple and roll into a lunchbag and ripped out of the house. Mom and Lucas had already left.

I raced for the bus. I took my seat and tried to relax, but my heart was still racing. Fifteen minutes later, we reached the school stop. I saw Liz walk into the building with Cheryl. She was too far away for me to call out to.

I walked up the stairs and into the building. Three kids were walking behind me.

They were whispering, but I could only catch a few words.

"No."

"Really?"

"Ohmygod! Is that what it said?"

I wondered what they were whispering about. I walked down the hall. Two girls who had been saying hi recently didn't say anything or even look at me. I suddenly felt invisible again.

I knew something was going on but what?

A crowd was milling around the lockers, talking and laughing, but as soon as I showed up the noise stopped dead.

A few kids coughed. A few others snapped their lockers shut and left. One girl gave me a strange look as if I had horns growing out of my head.

Something was definitely going on. Karin? Again? What new accusations had she made? What kind of trouble was

I in now? The peace I had felt in the previous few weeks evaporated as if it had never existed. I had to find Liz. She would know what was happening.

I raced to Liz's class right before lunch. I couldn't stand another minute of not knowing.

"Liz," I said when I saw her leaving class with Cheryl.

"Renata," the crack in her voice told me something awful had happened.

"What's up?" I asked. My voice was trembling.

"You don't have a computer do you?" asked Liz.

"No? Why?"

"Let's go to the library. I think you should see this. It's pretty...pretty... awful."

Liz's class was two doors from the library. We hurried inside. Liz turned on the nearest computer and quickly pulled up an image.

I stared at it. I thought I was going to throw up.

"I don't believe this," I said.

It was a picture of my mom with her head in a toilet bowl. Above the picture the words "Queen of the Toilet Bowl" were scrawled in bold black letters. Beside my mom's picture was a smaller one of me that read, "Like mother, like daughter."

My head felt like someone had spun me around and around. And then the pieces fell into place.

"Karin," I said.

"How did she get a picture of your mom?" asked Liz.

"My mom works for her bossy aunt, Ms. Powell. Karin was at her aunt's while my mom was there cleaning the house and, of course, the toilet too. Karin must have taken the picture and posted it."

"Wow," said Liz. "I can't believe she'd do that. I can't believe anyone would do that. It's one thing to be mean but this is beyond mean. What are we going to do?"

"We?" I mumbled.

"Of course, we, we're friends. Karin isn't going to get away with this."

"I don't know. I can't think. I know Karin wants me to fall apart and not play Maria. I know that's what this is all about. But what can I do? She'll deny all of this. Why does she have to be so mean? What did I do to her?"

"I found something out on Sunday that might explain everything."

"What?" I asked.

"Cheryl heard that Karin's dad ran off with their nanny from the Philippines about five years ago, and Karin has never forgiven her dad or her new stepmother."

"But I'm not from the Philippines," I said.

"Yes, but you are an immigrant. Just like the nanny. And Cheryl thinks Karin hates all immigrants. I mean it's a rotten deal to have your dad dump your mom for someone else, but that's no excuse to do this."

chapter fifteen

I wanted to hide. Anywhere. Under a desk, in the bathroom, at home. How could I walk down the halls at school after this?

I wanted to run, but I also wanted to scream at Karin. I wanted to tell her what I thought of her, make her feel what I was feeling.

"I can't go to class," I told Liz.

"You have to. You can't let Karin win. She wants you to feel miserable."

"Oh Liz," I said, swallowing hard, trying to stop the geyser of tears about to erupt from my eyes. "You're right. I should go to class, but I don't know if I can. I don't know how I'll get through today."

"You will," said Liz and she gave me a quick hug. "Gotta run. Remember, go to class. Stand tall. See you at lunch."

Maybe knowing that I would see Liz at lunch gave me the strength to go to class. At least at lunch, I wouldn't face everyone alone.

My next two classes were a blur. I tried not to notice the looks kids were giving me. I tried to keep focused on just sitting there, walking to class, not running away.

I made it to lunch.

"I knew you'd be here. I knew you'd make it," said Liz.

"Now what?" I said.

"The principal?" asked Liz.

"Yeah. Right. He's really going to believe me over Karin."

"But you know she was at Ms. Powell's. Your mother saw her," said Liz.

"You think Ms. Powell is going to say that Karin was there? Even if she does, Karin can still deny she did anything," I said.

"You might be right," said Liz. "But we can't let Karin get away with this."

"Look," I said, my head clearing for the first time that day. "Karin wants me to drop out of the show. I know that. If I don't, no matter how embarrassing the pictures are, she won't win. Right?"

"Right," said Liz. "So what you have to do is play it cool. Make believe you know nothing about the pictures."

"Or even...even...tell people you know someone took a nasty picture of your mom. Tell everyone she's a cleaning lady and someone made fun of her and is spreading it around the school."

"Yes!" said Liz, her face lighting up. "You don't even have to accuse Karin. Make what she did the terrible thing. You didn't do anything after all. Someone did something awful to you."

"But how do I do it?" I asked. "The principal is useless."

"But Ms. Watson is not. She plays things straight, and she knows what's going on at school. Also she's good friends with the vice principal."

"Let's talk to her after rehearsal," I said.

"You're on."

Somehow I got through the rest of the day. Knowing I had a plan helped. Knowing Liz was on my side helped. And knowing I hadn't done anything wrong helped even more.

At rehearsal I saw Karin looking at me, nudging her friends and raising her eyebrows. I ignored her as if she was a flea.

I sang. I spoke my lines. I got through the rehearsal. It took all my energy, but I got through it. And then Liz and I waited for everyone to leave so we could speak to Ms. Watson.

She'd already heard about the pictures.

"Renata, I have to tell you how shocked

and disgusted I am that someone would try to hurt you so much," she said. "Do you know who did this?"

"I have an idea but no proof," I said. "I can't let that picture hurt my family or me. My mother is a good person. "

"She's great," said Liz. "Pretty and smart and she bakes amazing cookies."

Ms. Watson laughed. "I'm looking forward to meeting her. I think we should make sure she isn't embarrassed at the show. Perhaps the staff should say something publicly about the picture. Would that make you feel more comfortable?"

"I'd like to say something too," I said.

"On stage?" Ms. Watson asked.

"Are you sure you want to?" asked Liz.

"I'm sure," I said.

"I think it's a terrific idea," said Ms. Watson. "It will put this whole thing out in public. You don't have to point a finger at anyone, just talk about what they did. Make the cruelty the shameful thing, not the picture. My guess is the perpetrator will not feel comfortable hearing you speak in public. And I bet you'll get a lot more kids supporting you than you think. It's not going to be easy, Renata. It's harder than standing up and acting in a show."

"I know," I said. "I'll do it."

"I'll speak to the vice principal and we'll see if we can call an assembly for tomorrow."

chapter sixteen

"Renata Nunes, please come to the office," said Ms. Bartlett during my first class the next morning.

A few kids looked up and gave me a "Boy are you in trouble" look as I left class.

I walked down the empty hall to the office. Was Ms. Watson able to arrange an assembly? Would the principal allow me to speak?

"Come in Renata," said Ms. Long, the vice principal. I'd never spoken to Ms. Long before, and I'd never noticed how tall she was before either. She was much taller than Mr. Bowman, who was nowhere to be seen.

"Mr. Bowman is out at a two-day conference," said Ms. Long. "I spoke to him briefly about the matter after Ms. Watson informed me of the situation. Mr. Bowman suggested I proceed as I see fit. So that's what I'm doing. I think Ms. Watson is correct. We need to address this horrible internet bullying. It's totally unacceptable."

"I know," I said, relieved Mr. Bowman was away and didn't care what the vice principal did.

"I'll call a short assembly this afternoon to address the issue. And if you are comfortable, I'd be happy to let you speak. But are you sure you want to get up on stage, Renata? It won't be easy."

"I want to," I said. "I just don't know what to say."

"Say what happened. Say what you feel. Your words will have more impact than anything I can say. Ms. Watson thinks the world of you, and she knows you can handle this."

Despite the shiver that was ripping through me like an electric shock, I smiled.

Thank you, Ms. Watson I thought, thank you.

"So we're on for two PM," said Ms. Long. "I'll speak first, then Ms. Watson and then you. Never forget that what you're doing takes courage, and what was done to you is the work of a coward and a bully."

For the rest of the morning, I kept rehearsing my words. For the rest of the morning, my knees shook like Jell-o Pops.

"I don't know if I can do this," I confided to Liz at lunch.

"Oh, Renata," said Liz. "You're being so brave. You're amazing. Remember I'll be in the audience cheering you on, and the vice principal and Ms. Watson are right behind you too."

"There will be a short assembly at two o'clock," an announcement suddenly boomed through the lunchroom.

"Another boring assembly," groaned three girls at a near-by table.

At ten to two, my class walked down to the auditorium. As we'd agreed, I walked over to Ms. Watson at the front and together we climbed the stairs to the stage.

The vice principal was already there, standing in the center of the stage.

From the corner of my eye, I saw Liz in the fourth row beside Cheryl. Liz gave me a quick thumbs-up.

Two rows behind her I saw Karin. She was staring at me. Did she sense what I was about to say? Was she scared? Did she care? I couldn't tell from her face. It was hard and unsmiling.

And what of the other kids? Would they hate me? Make fun of me? It was too late to change my mind now. I was up on stage.

Ms. Long was speaking. She made a statement denouncing the use of the internet to humiliate people. She said that she was outraged that a demeaning picture of a student and her mother had been posted on the internet. "This will not be tolerated in any way," she said. And then Ms. Watson spoke. She spoke slowly and clearly in her powerful voice. She didn't need a mike to be heard across the auditorium.

"The perpetrator of this act is a coward and a bully," she said. "We must all speak up when we see people hurting others. Bullying is cruel, even when it's not physical. Bullies must be stopped." And then Ms. Watson said, "Renata Nunes would like to address you now."

I walked to the microphone. I swallowed hard and then I spoke. The auditorium hushed to silence with my first words.

"My mother is a cleaning lady," I said. "She is a good, hard-working, kind person. I hope she never sees the picture of her that is posted on the internet or reads the words someone wrote to embarrass her and me. Whoever did this has no heart. No soul. No kindness. I am from Brazil, a beautiful country. I am proud of my mother. I am proud of who I am and where I'm from. That's all I have to say."

For the longest minute, there wasn't a sound in the auditorium. Then from the fourth row, where Cheryl and Liz sat, the applause began. It rippled, then grew and grew, and soon everyone was clapping.

The vice principal said, "Renata has shown great courage to stand before you today. If any of the staff discovers who did this, there will be dire consequences for that person. I hope never to have to deal with this kind of incident again. You may return to class."

"Renata, you were awesome," said Liz as we walked to our last class of the day.

"Boy am I lucky Mr. Bowman was away," I said. "I wonder what Karin will do now."

"I snuck a peek at her while you were speaking. She looked like she had turned into a bar of ice. I wonder how many kids know she did it."

"I wonder," I said. "But you now what? No matter what Karin does now, it doesn't matter. I spoke up. It's out there. I'm out there. No hiding."

"Well, after Friday, you won't be able to hide. You'll be a star!" said Liz.

chapter seventeen

After the assembly a few kids told me they thought it was great that I spoke up. Some kids said nothing, but I felt like something had changed. I felt like a load of rocks had been lifted off my back. I didn't want to hide any more.

Karin was absent for the next few days. Darleen said she had a bad cold, but Liz and I wondered if that was true. We wondered if Karin would even show up for the show. Ms. Watson suggested that Liz prepare for Karin's part, just in case.

Then it was the night of the show. By five o'clock, the whole cast was zipping around backstage, looking for clothes, rehearsing lines, popping buttons and calling for Ms. Watson's help. Ms. Watson zoomed around fixing broken zippers, finding lost clothes and helping calm nerves.

Everyone was there, except for Karin.

Liz was sure Karin wouldn't show up for the play. "She'll never come. She'll get her mom to call in with some excuse and then I'll have to do her part and fake the singing."

Liz, who was usually the coolest person I knew, who was never fazed by anything, looked like she'd been shot with an arrow.

"You'll manage. Don't worry. We'll all help you get through it," I told her.

"Easy for you to say. You sing like an angel. I sing like a frog. No, worse than a frog."

"Maybe you should get into the nun's costume," said Ms. Watson as she handed Liz Karin's outfit. But just as Liz was sliding into the long black skirt, Karin walked in.

"I was just about to call your house," said Ms. Watson. "I was afraid you wouldn't make it for the show. It's late."

"I wasn't feeling well," said Karin.

"Are you well enough now to go on?" asked Ms. Watson.

"Yes," said Karin.

"Then hurry into your costume. You don't have much time."

Liz almost leaped out of the costume and popped it into Karin's hand.

For a second, Karin and I looked at each other and then Karin hurried to the dressing room.

"I hear people," said Liz. "The audience is arriving."

Suddenly the dressing room was filled with panicked cries.

"Ohmygod."

"I'm not ready."

"What if I forget my lines?"

"My zipper is jammed."

"I hate my hair."

"You're all going to be fine," said Ms. Watson. "Everybody take a deep breath and remember we've rehearsed this. You know your lines. You're ready. Five minutes to show time."

Liz gave me a hug. "You are going to be the best Maria ever," she said.

"Thanks," I said.

"Break a leg," said Liz and she began to giggle.

"Thanks," I said laughing.

The music began. As I straightened my nun's habit, I saw my left shoelace was untied. I bent over to retie it.

When I stood up, Karin was standing beside me.

For an instant we looked at each other.

I smiled. "Break a leg," I told her.

"You too," said Karin, and she smiled back.

Then the curtain rose.

From that moment on everything was a dream. I sang, I rememebered my lines. I saw my mom's face glowing like a candle in church.

But the best part was when, without saying a word, the whole cast joined hands like we were one family. Then we bowed together as the audience stood up and cheered.

Frieda Wishinsky is the author of many popular books for children, including *A Bee in Your Ear, A Noodle Up Your Nose, Just Call Me Joe* and *Each One Special* Frieda lives with her family in Toronto, Ontario.

Also in the Orca Currents series

Camp Wild
by Pam Withers

"He's trying to portage the kayak by himself!" Herb exclaims. Before either of us can run forward to help him, Charlie stumbles. The earth beneath him gives way, and he and his boat tumble down in a small landslide. They hit the water above the falls with a splash.

"Rescue rope!" I scream.

Wilf is adamant that he is too old for summer camp. When his parents ignore his protests and ship him off anyway, he knows how he will get their attention: He will escape from camp by canoe and spend the rest of his vacation alone in the woods, proving to his parents he deserves his independence. His plan begins to unravel when his cabin mate forces Wilf to take him along. Things go from bad to worse when a younger camper follows them and they all end up in a fight for their lives against the unforgiving river.